James O. Halliwell-Phillipps

Memoranda on the Midsummer Night's Dream, A.D. 1879

and A.D. 1855

James O. Halliwell-Phillipps

Memoranda on the Midsummer Night's Dream, A.D. 1879 and A.D. 1855

ISBN/EAN: 9783337093129

Printed in Europe, USA, Canada, Australia, Japan

Cover: Foto ©Andreas Hilbeck / pixelio.de

More available books at **www.hansebooks.com**

MEMORANDA

Midsummer Night's Dream,

A.D. 1879 AND A.D. 1855.

BY

J. O. HALLIWELL-PHILLIPPS, F.R.S.

BRIGHTON :

PRINTED BY MESSRS. FLEET AND BISHOP.

———

1879.

THE "Introduction" reprinted at the close of these Memoranda was written by me in the year 1855. It is, I hope, unnecessary to observe that many of the opinions and arguments therein advanced are now seen to be untenable.

The most foolish perhaps of all of them is the form of contrast suggested between the Midsummer Night's Dream and Love's Labour's Lost, and taking it for granted that the latter must be an earlier composition. It may certainly be so, but Love's Labour's Lost was probably written *in its amended form* in the year 1597, and first acted *in that state* before Queen Elizabeth in the Christmas holidays of that year. There is no good evidence that the Midsummer Night's Dream was written any length of time before the month of September, 1598, at which period it is mentioned by Meres under the title of *Midsummers night dreame*.

The accounts of the bad weather of 1594 are valueless in the question of the chronology, and, indeed, as Mr. Knight has observed,

Stowe's notice of the " fair harvest" in August is inconsistent with Titania's description. Let us hope that the following new evidence derived from Spenser may be considered to be of a more decisive character.

It is this. There seems to be a certainty that Shakespeare, in the composition of the Midsummer Night's Dream, had in one place a recollection of the sixth book of the Faerie Queene, published in 1596, for he all but lite-rally quotes the following line from the eighth canto of that book,—" *Through hils and dales, through bushes and through breres,*" Faerie Queene, ed. 1596, p. 460. As the Midsummer Night's Dream was not printed until the year 1600, and it is impossible that Spenser could have been present at any representation of the comedy before he had written the sixth book of the Faerie Queene, it may fairly be concluded that Shakspeare's play was not composed at the earliest before the year 1596, in fact, not until some time after January the 20th, 1595-6, on which day the Second Part of the Faerie Queene was entered on the books of the Sta-tioners' Company. The sixth book of that poem was probably written as early as 1592 or 1593, certainly in Ireland and at some con-

siderable time before the month of November,
1594, the date of the entry of publication of
the Amoretti, in the eightieth sonnet of which
it is distinctly alluded to as having been com-
pleted previously to the composition of the
latter work.

The following passage in the comedy of the
Wisdome of Doctor Dodypoll, 1600,—

> 'Twas I that lead you through the painted meades,
> Where the light fairies daunst upon the flowers,
> Hanging on every leafe an orient pearle,
> Which, strooke together with the silken winde,
> Of their loose mantels made a silver chime,

has been thought to have been imitated from
the Midsummer Night's Dream. As Dr. Dodi-
powle is mentioned by Nash as early as 1596,
this argument would prove Shakespeare's comedy
to have been then in existence ; but surely the
imagery is too vague for such a conclusion to
be safely arrived at. In all these discussions
we should be careful to exclude the reception of
evidence from similarities of language that
might by any possibility be accidental. This
can scarcely be the case with the coincidence
above cited from Spenser.

According to Mr. Stokes, who derives his information from books with which I am not

acquainted,—" Elze, Kurz and Dowden think the Midsummer Night's Dream was written to do honour to the marriage of the Earl of Essex in 1590," Attempt to Determine the Chronological Order, 1878, p. 48. A variety of similar conjectures, equally gratuitous and equally silly, are mentioned in the same elegant and useful work.

In reference to Mr. Gerald Massey's opinion that " Shakespeare unquestionably borrowed from Drayton's Nymphidia to enrich his fairy world of the Midsummer Night's Dream," it may be well to observe that there is no doubt that Drayton's poem was written after the publication of the comedy. Bindley, the celebrated collector, possessed a copy of Drayton's Battaile of Agincourt, Miseries of Queen Margarite, Nimphidia, &c., fol. Lond. 1627, with the following manuscript note in the author's own handwriting,—" to the noble knight, my most honored frend, Sir Henry Willoughby, one of the selected patrons of *thes my latest poems,* from his servant, Mi. Drayton."

The woodcut on the title-page of Fisher's edition of the Midsummer Night's Dream, 1600, is the printer's device. It is repeated in the second part of Antonio's Revenge, " Printed for Thomas Fisher, and are to be soulde in Saint Dunstans Church-yard, 1602." It may be just worth notice that the wood-block used on the title-page of Roberts's edition of the Midsummer Night's Dream, 1600, was slightly cracked.

"A Midsommers Nights Dreame, comedie," occurs in a list of books read by Drummond of Hawthornden in the year 1606, a list of which is preserved in manuscript in the library of the Society of Antiquaries of Edinburgh. The play is also named by him in a list of books in his possession in the year 1611.

It should be mentioned that the comedy of the Fleire, which furnishes so curious an illustration of the character of Thisbe as represented in Shakespeare's time, was entered on the books of the Stationers' Company in May, 1606, as, "A Comedie called the Fleare."

Unless the sentence was a proverbial one, Sir T. Hoby must be considered to quote the Midsummer Night's Dream in a letter to Mr. T. H., 1609,—"And yet let mee tell you this, *for ought that ever I could reade*, there is no such great difference betweene our practise and S. Augustines custome as you surmise."

As the following lines in the Night-Raven by
Samuel Rowlands, 1620,—

> I take a notice what your youth are doing,
> When you are fast asleepe how they are wooing,
> And steale together by some secret call,
> Like Piramus and Thisby through the wall,

occur shortly after an allusion to the old play
of Hamlet, it is allowable to conjecture that
the acting comedy of the Midsummer Night's
Dream was in the writer's thoughts.

It appears from a stage-direction in the first
folio edition of 1623 that a player named
Tawyer headed the procession of the actors
in the interlude as trumpeter. This direction
proves that the editors of the folio used a play-
house copy of the Midsummer Night's Dream,
perhaps, however, a printed edition noted for
the stage. William Tawyer was a subordinate
actor in the Globe Theatre in the pay of
Heminges.

The interlude of Pyramus and Thisbe may
have been separately performed at a very early
period. This at least may perhaps be inferred
from the following curious notice in Gee's New
Shreds of the Old Snare, 1624, — "as for
flashes of light, we might see very cheape
in the Comedie of Piramus and Thisbe, where

one comes in with a lanthorne and acts
Mooneshine." Charles the First, in his copy
of the second folio of 1632 preserved at
Windsor Castle, writes " Piramus and Thisby "
as if it were a second title to Shakespeare's
comedy, and the popularity of the Clown
portion of the Midsummer Night's Dream
in the seventeenth century is well illustrated
by the following curious extract from Tate's
farce of Cuckold's Haven, or an Alderman
no Conjuror, 1685, — " *Wyn.* Ay, but there
is a pretty play in Moorfields.—*Sec.* Why, I
will act thee a better play myself. What wilt
thou have ? The Knight of the Burning
Pestle or the Doleful Comedy of Piramus and
Thisbe ? That's my masterpiece. When Piramus comes to be dead, I can act a dead man
rarely ! The rageing rocks, and shivering
shocks, shall break the locks of prison gates ;
and Phœbus carr shall shine from far, to make
and marr, the foolish fates. Was not that lofty
now ? Then there's the Lion, Wall and Moon-
shine, three heroick parts ; I play'd 'em all at
school. I roard'd out the Lion so terribly that
the company call'd out to me to roar again."

The transformation of Bottom was probably
familiar to Shakspeare as introduced upon the

stage. One of the stage-directions in the Chester Mysteries is,—" then Balaham shall strike his asse, and remark that here it is necessary for some one to be transformed into the appearance of an asse." Compare also the account of the acting of the Elizabethan play of the Cradle of Security, in Willis's Mount Tabor, 1639,—"the play was called the Cradle of Security, wherin was personated a king or some great prince, with his courtiers of severall kinds, amongst which three ladies were in speciall grace with him ; and they, keeping him in delights and pleasures, drew him from his graver counsellors, hearing of sermons, and listning to good counsell and admonitions, that in the end they got him to lye down in a cradle upon the stage, where these three ladies joyning in a sweet song rocked him asleepe that he snorted againe ; and in the meane time closely conveyed under the cloaths wherewithall he was covered a vizard, like a swines snout, upon his face, with three wire chaines fastned thereunto, the other end whereof being holden severally by those three ladies, who fall to singing againe, and then discovered his face that the spectators might see how they had transformed him, going on with their singing."

At the time of the composition of the Midsummer Night's Dream our great dramatist was certainly acquainted with the Life of Theseus in North's translation of Plutarch, whence he took the corrupted form of the name of Ægle, spelt *Eagles* in the old editions of the play, and *Ægles* in North. Other names are taken from the same work. The Perigenia of the comedy may be a printer's error for the Perigouna of the author's manuscript, the latter form being that found in the English version of Plutarch.

Charles Lamb, in a manuscript that I have seen, speaks of Shakespeare as having "invented the fairies ;" by which, I presume, he means that his refinement of the popular notion of them was sufficiently expansive to justify the strong epithet.

What is absurdly termed æsthetic criticism is more out of place on this comedy than perhaps on any other of Shakespeare's plays. It deadens the "native wood-notes wild" that every reader of taste would desire to be left to their own influences. The Midsummer Night's Dream is too exquisite a composition to be dulled by the infliction of philosophical analysis.

J. O. H.-P.

Hollingbury Copse, Brighton,
26 August, 1879.

THE earliest recorded notice of the Midsummer Night's Dream is found in the Palladis Tamia of Meres, published in the year 1598, where it is classed with other comedies, the composition of which is generally referred to the commencement of Shakespeare's career of dramatic authorship. Any opinion respecting the length of time this play had been before the public, previously to the mention of it by that writer, must necessarily be formed solely upon conjecture, the presumed allusions to contemporary events being scarcely entitled to assume the dignity of evidences. Amongst the latter, the spirited account of the ungenial seasons resulting from the quarrels of Titania and Oberon may perhaps be considered the most important; and it must be admitted that such a description would have had a peculiar application, were the comedy first written soon after the extraordinary summer of 1594, when the severity of the weather was sufficiently singular to have attracted the marked notice of contemporary writers. The reader will observe how

nearly some of their accounts coincide with
Titania's description. Dr. Forman, the celebrated astrologer, in an original MS. in the
Ashmolean Museum (No. 384), has preserved
the following notes of the year 1594,—"Ther
was moch sicknes but lyttle death, moch fruit
and many plombs of all sorts this yeare and
small nuts, but fewe walnuts: this monethes of
June and July wer very wet and wonderfull
cold like winter, that the 10. dae of Julii many
did syt by the fyer, yt was so cold; and soe
was yt in Maye and June; and scant too faire
dais together all that tyme, but yt rayned every
day more or lesse: yf yt did not raine, then
was yt cold and cloudye: there wer many
gret fludes this sommer, and about Michelmas,
thorowe the abundaunce of raine that fell so-
deinly, the brige of Ware was broken downe,
and at Stratford Bowe, the water was never
sine so byg as yt was; and in the lattere end of
October, the waters burste downe the bridg at
Cambridge, and in Barkshire wer many gret
waters, wherwith was moch harm done so-
denly." The floods of this year are mentioned by several other writers. "This yere,"
says Stowe the Chronicler, "in the month of
May, fell many great showers of rain, but in

the months of June and July much more; for it commonly rained every day or night till St. James' day, and two days after together most extremely; all which notwithstanding, in the month of August, there followed a fair harvest, but in the month of September fell great rains, which raised high waters, such as stayed the carriages, and broke down bridges at Cambridge, Ware, and elsewhere in many places," a statement which is copied into Penkethman's Artachthos, 1638. There are also some curious notices of this season in Dr. King's Lectures upon Jonas delivered at Yorke in the yeare of our Lorde 1594,—" Remember that the spring was very unkind, by means of the abundance of rains that fell; our July hath been like to a February; our June even as an April; so that the air must needs be corrupted: God amend it in his mercy, and stay this plague of waters!" Then, having spoken of three successive years of scarcity, he adds,—" and see, whether the Lord doth not threaten us much more, by sending such unseasonable weather and storms of rain among us, which if we will observe, and compare it with that which is past, we may say that the course of nature is very much inverted; our years are turned upside down; our summers

are no summers ; our harvests are no harvests ;
our seeds-times are no seeds-times : for a great
space of time, scant any day hath been seen
that it hath not rained upon us ; and the nights
are like the days." This account, which bears
a remarkable analogy to a portion of the speech
of Titania, refers entirely to the year 1594.
The following extract from the same work, with
which these notices may be concluded, alludes,
according to the marginal remark, to 1593 and
1594 ;—" The moneths of the year have not
yet gone about, wherin the Lorde hath bowed
the heavens, and come downe amongst us with
more tokens and earnests of his wrath intended,
then the agedst man of our lande is able to re-
count of so small a time ; for say if ever the
windes, since they blew one against the other,
have beene more common and more tempestu-
ous, as if the foure ends of heaven had con-
spired to turne the foundations of the earth
upside downe ; thunders and lightnings neither
seasonable for the time, and withall most ter-
rible, with such effectes brought forth, that the
childe unborne shall speake of it : the anger of
the clouds hath beene powred downe upon our
heades, both with abundance, and, saving to
those that felt it, with incredible violence."

Evidences of this description, employed in the attempt to determine the real date of composition, are at the best chiefly valuable when adduced as corroborative of an opinion derived from other considerations. In the present instance, the period indicated by the allusion to the weather, which would lead to the supposition that the comedy was first produced either towards the close of the year 1594, or early in 1595, agrees very well with the internal evidence afforded by the play itself, which, although highly finished, scarcely exhibits the extent of genius displayed even in Love's Labour's Lost, a production which is acknowledged by general consent to be an early composition. It may, indeed, be objected to this view, that the elaboration rather than the power of the efforts of Shakespeare's genius is a better argument for its appropriation to a later period of the chronology; but there is always this difficulty in considering the progress of a mind so extensive in its grasp that the inferior intellects of all those who attempt to pass a judgment upon this most obscure inquiry, cannot, by any sensible approximation, estimate the improbability of a high work of art having been produced by Shakespeare within a very short interval after the composition of another which, in comparison, can merely be fairly described as a more careless study, even although it may be superior to the other as a work of genius.

The obscure allusion in the fifth act to the nine Muses lamenting " the death of learning," unless it be considered to have a general application to the decline of the more serious literature, may be accepted as the next most important evidence hitherto adduced in the question of the chronology. This is generally considered to refer to some author of the time, whose closing days were passed in indigence ; on which supposition, the conjecture of Mr. Knight, that Robert Greene was the person indicated by Shakespeare, bears great appearance of probability, the career of that writer agreeing in several particulars with the allusions in the comedy. The miserable death of Greene in September, 1592, was a subject of general conversation for several years, and a reference to the circumstance, though indistinctly expressed, would have been well understood in literary circles at the time it is supposed the comedy was produced. " Truely I have beene ashamed," observes Harvey, speaking of the last days of Greene, " to heare some ascertayned reportes of

hys most woefull and rascall estate ; how the
wretched fellow, or shall I say the Prince of
Beggars, laid all to gage for some few shillinges ;
and was attended by lice ; and would pittifully
beg a penny pott of Malmesie ; and could not
gett any of his old acquaintance to comfort or
visite him in his extremity but Mistris Appleby,
and the mother of Infortunatus," Four Letters
and certaine Sonnets, 1592. And again, in the
same work,—" his hostisse Isam, with teares in
her eies, and sighes from a deeper fountaine, for
she loved him derely, tould me of his lamentable
begging of a penny pott of Malmesy, and how
he was faine, poore soule, to borrow her hus-
bandes shirte, whiles his owne was a washing ;
and how his dublet and hose and sword were
sold for three shillinges." This testimony, although emanating from an ill-wisher, is not con-
troverted by the statements of Nash, who had
not the same opportunity of obtaining correct
information; and, on the whole, it cannot be
doubted that Greene "deceased in beggary."
His " learning " was equally notorious. " For
judgement Jove, for learning deepe he still
Apollo seemde," Greenes Funeralls, 1594.
There is nothing in the consideration that the
poet had been attacked by Greene as the " up-

start crow," to render Mr. Knight's theory im-
probable. The allusion in the comedy, if ap-
plicable to Greene, was certainly not conceived
in an unkind spirit ; and the death of one who
at most was probably rather jealous than bitterly
inimical, under such afflicting circumstances,
there can be no doubt would have obliterated
all trace of animosity from a mind so generous
as was that of Shakespeare.

Other critics have believed that Spenser was
the individual alluded to in the above-mentioned
passage, but the period of his death, which did
not take place till early in the year 1599, pre-
cludes the possibility of this opinion being
correct, unless the forced explanation, that the
lines were inserted after the first publication, be
adopted. There is greater probability in the
supposition that there is a reference to Spenser's
poem, the Teares of the Muses, which appeared
in 1591, in which the nine Muses are introduced
sorrowing for the decay of learning, the same
poem, it will be remembered, in which " our
pleasant Willy " is lamented as being "dead
of late ; " but the words of Shakespeare certainly appear to be more positive in their application. There can be little doubt that the
circumstances of Spenser were embarrassed

shortly previous to his death, but there was assistance available, and he can scarcely be stated with certainty to have "deceased in beggary." The circumstances were these : The Irish of Munster rising in October, 1598, laid waste the country, and expelled the English, Spenser being included in the list of those who were compelled to return to England with ruined fortunes. It appears that he then lodged at Westminster, where he died in the January of the following year, the expenses of his funeral being defrayed by the Earl of Essex. Ben Jonson, in his conversations with William Drummond, asserts that Spenser "died for lake of bread in King Street, and refused twenty pieces sent to him by my Lord of Essex, and said he was sorrie he had no time to spend them." This looks somewhat as if there were exaggeration in the first statement. It is, however, fair to observe that a similar story is related by Lane, in his Triton's Trumpet, a manuscript bearing the date of 1621, with this essential distinction, that another hand had, previously to his Lordship's offer, sent him "crownes good store." Spenser was also in receipt of a pension from the Queen, which does not appear to have lapsed before his decease.

As far as is at present known, the plot of the Midsummer Night's Dream is one of the very few invented by Shakespeare himself. It is true that a few slight portions of the ground-work are derived from other sources, but the tale and its construction are believed to be original. The translation of Plutarch's life of Theseus, and Chaucer's Knight's Tale, appear to have furnished little more than the names of the characters ; but it is just possible that the following passage, at the close of the latter, may have suggested the introduction of the interlude of the clowns :—

> ————ne how the Grekes play
> The wake plaies ne kepe I not to say :
> Who wrestled best naked with oile enoint,
> Ne who that bare him best in no disjoint.
> I woll not tellen eke how they all gon
> Hom till Athenes, whan the play is don.

Golding's translation of Ovid has better claims to the honour of having been used by Shakespeare in the construction of a part of his play, the similarities between the tale of Pyramus and Thisbe in that work and the interlude being sufficiently striking to warrant the belief of its being the original source of the latter. The poet seems also to have been indebted for a casual expression to Chaucer's Legende of

Thisbe of Babylon ; but no source has yet been indicated, which leads to the opinion that anything beyond the merest outline of the introduction of the historical characters, and the subject of the interlude performed by the clowns, was obtained from any older production.

The story of Pyramus and Thisbe was very familiar to an Elizabethan audience, not merely in translations of Ovid, but as having been told in prose and verse by numerous English writers of the sixteenth century. It is related in the Boke of the Cyté of Ladies, 4to. 1521 ; and in a very rare poetical work, La Conusaunce d'Amours, printed by Pynson. William Griffith, in 1562-3, obtained a "lycense for pryntinge of a boke intituled Perymus and Thesbye," published in quarto for T. Hackett. The history of Pyramus and Thisby, "truly translated," is given in the Gorgeous Gallery of Gallant Inventions, 1578, and in A Handefull of Pleasant Delites by Clement Robinson, 1584, there is "a new sonet of Pyramus and Thisbie." Dunston Gale, in 1596, wrote a poem called Pyramus and Thisbe, the earliest known printed edition of which appeared in 1617. There is no allusion in it to A Midsummer Night's Dream. The story is also told in the

Silkewormes and their Flies, by T. M., 4to.
Lond. 1599, in verse; in Topsell's Historie of
Fourc-Footed Beasts, 1607, p. 472; and it
would appear from a passage in Gayton's Notes
upon Don Quixote, 1654, p. 16, that there was
an old popular chap-book history of Pyramus
and Thisbe, it being mentioned in company
with the Unfortunate Lover and Argalus and
Parthenia. Compare also the following extract
from Dame Dobson or the Cunning Woman,
1684,—"You are in the right, I have read some
such thing in Pyramus and the Seven Cham-
pions, and Valentine and Orson."

The main action of this comedy is supported
neither by the classical personages nor by the
clowns, but by the fairies. Without the last, the
play would be an insignificant skeleton. Deprived of the dramatic contrast furnished by the
proceedings of the clowns, it would have partaken too greatly of the character of a masque;
but these must be considered, in any view of
the case, to be subservient to the action of the
fairies. These latter, as Shakespeare has treated
them, are unquestionably derived from English
sources. The poet has founded his elfin world
on the prettiest of the people's traditions, and
has clothed them with the ever-living flowers of

his own exuberant fancy. How much in reality is the invention of Shakspeare is difficult to ascertain; and his successors have rendered the subject more obscure by adopting the graceful world he has created, as though it had been interwoven with the popular mythology, and formed a part of it. There can, however, be no doubt that the main characteristics of the fairies, as they are delineated in the present comedy, were taken directly from the ordinary superstitions of the time. Tales of Robin Goodfellow are mentioned, more than once in Scot's Discoverie of Witchcraft, first published in 1584. Nash, in his Terrors of the Night, 1594, observes that "the Robin Goodfellowes, elfes, fairies, hobgoblins of our latter age, did most of their merry prankes in the night : then ground they malt, and had hempen shirts for their labours, daunst in greene meadows, pincht maids in their sleep that swept not their houses cleane, and led poor travellers out of their way notoriously." In Tarlton's Newes out of Purgatorie, published a few years previously, we are told that Robin Goodfellow was "famozed in every old wives chronicle for his mad merrye prankes." It is, therefore, possible that the rare prose tract, Robin Good-fellow his mad

Prankes and merry Jests, the earliest known edition of which is dated in 1628, was either written before the publication of the Midsummer Night's Dream, or at least that it was formed upon popular tradition. The latter suggestion is probably the true one, and, if so, the work is of singular interest as exhibiting, what might have been expected, the more prominent qualities of the Robin Goodfellow of Shakespeare in a coarser form, and of course in one less adapted for the poetical accompaniments by which he is surrounded in the comedy. The fairies of the tract are thus introduced,— "Once upon a time, a great while agoe, when men did eate more and drinke lesse,—then men were more honest, that knew no knavery then some now are, that confesse the knowledge and deny the practise—about that time (when so ere it was) there was wont to walke many harmlesse spirits called fayries, dancing in brave order in fayry rings on greene hills with sweet musicke (sometime invisible) in divers shapes ; many mad prankes would they play, as pinching of sluts black and blue, and misplacing things in ill-ordered houses ; but lovingly would they use wenches that cleanly were, giving them silver and other pretty toyes, which they would leave for them, sometimes in their **shooes**, other times in their pockets, sometimes in bright basons and other **cleane** vessels." Some of Robin's **own** adventures are very similar to those **described by himself in the** play, **as amongst his** favourite amusements ; **and a few of his tricks** and transformations **are** identical with some that are mentioned **in** the latter.

The introduction of the popular fairy mythology **of** England into a drama, the events **of** which are supposed to occur in the classical period of Greece, appears on the first consideration to exhibit a singular incongruity, **one** which might be presumed to require the apology suggested by the title of a dream. But it **may** well be questioned whether this apparent inconsistency is not intentional on the part **of** the author, and whether the scene of **action might not** have been purposely removed **into a distant** age for the purpose of reconciling the **educated** spectator to the introduction of the fairy characters. The belief in fairies was unquestionably general amongst the less advanced classes of society in Shakespeare's time, **but** there is great reason to suspect that this popular faith was not so deeply rooted as was that in **witchcraft,** and it may fairly be considered, in

support of the above view of the subject, that
the poet's audience would number many who
would have turned into ridicule a domestic
English comedy of the time in which the
fairies constituted a serious and prominent part
of the action. The objection usually raised
against the choice of the title of the play, that
the dream occurred on the eve of May-day,
and not at Midsummer, really shows that the
name was not adopted solely in relation to
the comedy itself, or with special reference to
the presumed incongruity resulting from the
introduction of the fairies. There is greater
probability that it was first produced upon the
stage in June, perhaps before the Court on
Midsummer Night; in the same way that the
Winter's Tale, the action of which is laid at the
time of sheep-shearing, is most likely indebted
for its title to the period when it was brought
out. Aubrey, in his MS. account of Shakespeare preserved in the Ashmolean Museum, in
a blundering paragraph relating to the Midsummer Night's Dream, suggests that the title
of this comedy was taken from the circumstance
that a character in it was copied from a constable
whom the poet met with at a village in Bucking-
hamshire, when he happened to be sojourning

there on a Midsummer Night. His words are,—
"The humour of . . . . the cunstable in a
Midsomer's Night's Dreame, he happened to
take at Grenden in Bucks (I thinke it was Midsomer Night that he happened to lye there)
which is the roade from London to Stratford,
and there was living that constable about 1642,
when I first came to Oxon : Mr. Jos. Howe
is of the parish, and knew him." The assertion of Aubrey respecting Shakespeare having
stopped at this place on Midsummer Night is
probably conjectural; and there is an evident
mistake in the story, no constable being introduced into the play. He may possibly have
meant the comedy of Much Ado about Nothing,
and referred to the character of Dogberry.

The choice of the time of new moon for the
nuptials of Theseus creates an anachronism,
when the hard-handed actors assert that the
moon shines on the night they exhibit their
play. Other oversights of a like kind may also
deserve notice. The period of action is four
days, concluding with the night of the new
moon. But Hermia and Lysander receive the
edict of Theseus four days before the new
moon; they fly from Athens "to-morrow
night;" they become the sport of the fairies,

along with Helena and Demetrius, *during one
night only*, for, Oberon accomplishes all in one
night, **before** "the first cock crows;" **and the**
lovers are discovered by Theseus the morning
before that which would have rendered this
portion **of** the plot chronologically consistent.
For, although Oberon, addressing **his** queen,
says,—

> **Now thou** and I are **new** in **amity,**
> And will, *to-morrow midnight*, solemnly
> **Dance** in Duke Theseus' house triumphantly.

yet Theseus, when he discovers the lovers, asks
Egeus,—" is not this **the** day that Hermia
should give answer of **her** choice ?," and the
answer of Egeus, " It **is,** my Lord," coupled
with what Theseus says **to** Hermia in the first
Act—" Take time to pause ; and by the next new
moon," &c., proves that **the** action **of** the re-
maining **part of the** play **is not intended to** consist of two days. The preparation **and** rehearsal
of the interlude present similar inconsistencies.
In Act i., Sc. 2, Quince is the only one who has
any knowledge of the " most lamentable comedy,
and most cruel death of Pyramus and Thisbe,"
and he selects actors for Thisbe's mother,
Pyramus's father, and Thisbe's **father, none** of
whom appear in the interlude **itself.** In Act iii.,

Sc. 1, there is the commencement of the play in rehearsal, none of which appears in the piece itself. Again, the play could have been but partially rehearsed once; for Bottom only returns in time to advise "every man look o'er his part;" and immediately before his companions were lamenting the failure of their "sport." How then could the "merry tears" of Philostrate be shed at its rehearsal?

The Midsummer Night's Dream was entered on the books of the Stationers' Company on October 8th, 1600,—" Tho: ffysher,—a booke called a Mydsomer Nightes Dreame, vj.d." Fisher, the publisher of this edition, issued it to the public before the close of the year, under the following title,—" A Midsommer nights dreame.—As it hath beene sundry times publickely acted by the Right honourable the Lord Chamberlaine his servants. Written by William Shakespeare.—Imprinted at London for Thomas Fisher, and are to be soulde at his shoppe at the Signe of the White Hart in Fleetestreete, 1600." Fisher's device of a halcyon with a fish in its mouth is inserted in the lower portion of the title, and he was possibly also the printer of the volume. Another edition, printed by Roberts, also appeared in the same year, entitled,—"A Midsommer nights dreame.—As it hath beene sundry times publikely acted by the Right Honourable the Lord Chamberlaine his servants.—Written by William Shakespeare.—Printed by James Roberts, 1600." It is a curious circumstance that, although there are a sufficient number of textual variations to warrant the conjecture that these editions are derived from separate sources, there appears to be an imitation of typical arrangement leading to the opinion that, in reality, one was copied in some degree from the other; and perhaps Fisher's edition, which, on the whole, seems to be more correct than the other, was printed from a corrected copy of that published by Roberts. It has, indeed, been usually supposed that Fisher's edition was the earliest, but no evidence has been adduced in support of this assertion, and the probabilities are against this view being the correct one. Fisher's edition could not have been published till nearly the end of the year, and, in the absence of direct information to the contrary, it may be presumed that the one printed by Roberts is really the first edition.

There are reasons for believing that, notwithstanding the general opinion of the unfitness of the Midsummer Night's Dream for representation, it was a successful acting play in the seventeenth century. An obscure comedy, at least, would scarcely have furnished Sharpham with the following exceedingly curious allusion, evidently intended as one that would be familiar to the audience, which occurs in his play of the Fleire, published in 1607,—" *Kni*. And how lives he with 'am ?—*Fle*. Faith, like Thisbe in the play, 'a has almost kil'd himselfe with the scabberd,"—a notice which is also valuable as recording a fragment belonging to the history of the original performance of Shakespeare's comedy, the interlude of the clowns, it may be concluded, having been conducted in the extreme of burlesque, and the actor who represented Thisbe, when he pretends to kill himself, falling upon the scabbard instead of upon the sword. The Midsummer Night's Dream is again noticed in an interesting passage in the Sir Gregory Nonsence of John Taylor, first published in 1622, a ridiculous medley in which, say the author,—" if the printer hath placed any line, letter or sillable, whereby this large volume may be made guilty to be understood by any man, I would have the reader not to impute the fault to the author, for it was farre from his purpose to write to any purpose, so

ending at the beginning, I say, as it is applawse-
fully written and commended to posterity in the
Midsummer nights dreame,—If we offend, it is
with our good will, we came with no intent, but
to offend, and show our simple skill." The
honest Water-Poet, probably quoting from
memory, has not followed the text of the play
very correctly, but the notice is valuable as an
additional evidence of the popularity of the
comedy, and especially of that portion of it
represented by the clowns. The next extrinsic
allusion to the play was discovered by Mr.
Collier in a manuscript at Lambeth Palace,
which gives a very singular account of a play
represented at the Bishop of Lincoln's house on
the night of Sunday, September 27th, 1631.
The piece chosen for this occasion was the
Midsummer Night's Dream, and it was got up
as a private amusement; but the Puritans
exerted their influence to punish this breach of
the due observance of the Sabbath, or rather
perhaps made it an important cause of com-
plaint against the Bishop; and the following
order is extracted from a decree made by a self-
constituted court, which partakes of something
of the satirical, and may have been written to
perpetuate the scandal rather than with any

more serious purpose,—" Likewise wee doe order that Mr. Wilson, because hee was a speciall plotter and contriver of this business, and did in such a brutishe manner acte the same with an asses head, and therefore hee shall, uppon Tuisday next, from six of the clocke in the morning till six of the clocke at night, sitt in the Porter's Lodge at my Lords Bishopps House, with his feete in the stocks, and attyred with his asse head, and a bottle of hay sett before him, and this subscription on his breast :—

> " Good people, I have played the beast,
>   And brought ill things to passe :
> I was a man, but thus have made
>   Myselfe a silly asse."

Bottom appears to have been then considered the most prominent character in the play ; and " the merry conceited humors of Bottom the Weaver," with a portion of the fairy scenes, were extracted from the Midsummer Night's Dream, and made into a farce or droll (The Merry conceited Humors of Bottom the Weaver, as it hath been often publikely acted by some of his Majesties Comedians, and lately privately presented by several apprentices for their harmless recreation, with great applause, 4to. Lond.

1661), which was very frequently played "on the sly" after the suppression of the theatres. "When the publique theatres were shut up," observes Kirkman, "and the actors forbidden to present us with any of their tragedies, because we had enough of that in ernest; and comedies, because the vices of the age were too lively and smartly represented; then all that we could divert ourselves with were these humours and pieces of plays, which passing under the name of a merry conceited fellow called Bottom the Weaver, Simpleton the Smith, John Swabber, or some such title, were only allowed us, and that but by stealth too, and under pretence of rope-dancing and the like," The Wits, 4to. Lond. 1673, an abridgement of Kirkman's Wits, or Sport upon Sport, 8vo. Lond. 1672. Both these contain the Humors of Bottom the Weaver, in which Puck is transformed by name into Pugg. The Midsummer Night's Dream, in its integrity, did not please generally after the Restoration. Pepys, who saw it acted in September, 1662, does not scruple to condemn its insipidity,—" To the King's Theatre, where we saw Midsummer Night's Dream, which I had never seen before, nor shall ever again, for it is the most insipid ridiculous play that ever I saw

in my life." Yet this condemnatory criticism
was equalled, if not excelled, by Lord Orford
in the following century, the latter writer observing, in a letter to Bentley, dated in 1755,
on the occasion of the production of Garrick's
alteration,—"Garrick has produced a detestable
English opera, which is crowded by all true
lovers of their country ; to mark the opposition
to Italian operas, it is sung by some cast singers,
two Italians, and a French girl, and the Chapel
boys ; and to regale us with sense, it is Shakespeare's Midsummer Night's Dream, which is
forty times more nonsensical than the worst
translation of any Italian opera-books." The
earlier alteration above mentioned, the Humors
of Bottom the Weaver, certainly met with success when it was represented. The publishers
of the edition of 1661, Francis Kirkman and
Henry Marsh, observe in their address to the
reader,—"the entreaty of several persons, our
friends, hath enduced us to the publishing of
this piece, which, when the life of action was
added to it, pleased generally well." And again,
—" supposing that things of this nature will
be acceptable, have therefore begun with this,
which we know may be easily acted, and may be

now as fit for a private recreation, as formerly it hath been for a publike."

The comic portions of this drama were also separately produced upon the German stage in the seventeenth century, and, if we may give credence to Gryphius, they were adapted by Daniel Schwenter, who died in 1636, and introduced by him, of course before that period, on the stage at Altorff. The Absurda Comica oder Herr Peter Squentz of Andreas Gryphius was published at Leipsic in 1663, and is a curious paraphrastical adaptation of the comic scenes of Shakespeare's play; but the author claims another origin for the story he has adopted, observing, in his address to the reader, —" I herewith present to thee Peter Squenz, a name not unknown in Germany : although all his devices are not so ingenious as he thinks for, yet they have been well received on various stages, and have caused no little merriment to the spectators ; but lest he should any longer be indebted to foreigners for his origin, be it known unto thee that Daniel Schwenter, the man who deserves well of all Germany, and is skilled in all sorts of languages as well as in the mathematical sciences, first introduced him on the stage at Altorff, and thence he has travelled over the length and breadth of the country." If Gryphius was really unacquainted with Shakespeare's drama, it is evident that he was indebted to some early German adaptation of it; and there is no improbability in the supposition that Schwenter introduced the comedy on the German stage, although unfortunately no copy of his version has yet been discovered.

In the year 1692, the Midsummer Night's Dream was changed into an opera under the title of the Fairy Queen, and performed at Dorset Garden. This alteration was printed at London the same year, and was produced on a very splendid scale. "In ornament," says Downes, "it was superior, especially in cloaths, for all the singers and dancers, scenes, machines and decorations, all most profusely set off and excellently performed, chiefly the instrumental and vocal part composed by Mr. Purcel, and dances by Mr. Priest. The court and town were wonderfully satisfied with it; but the expenses in setting it being so great, the company got very little by it." It was printed in 4to, 1692 and 1693. Richard Leveridge, in 1716 (published, 12mo. Lond.), adapted from this play A Comick Masque of Pyramus and Thisbe, which was produced at the theatre in Lincoln's

Inn Fields ; and in 1745, appeared a mock opera of Pyramus and Thisbe, set to music by Mr. Lampe, and acted at Covent Garden, 8vo. Lond. 1745, also taken from this comedy.

In 1755, Garrick produced, at Drury Lane, an opera taken from the Midsummer Night's Dream, under the title of The Fairies (published at London, 8vo. 1755). The parts of the clowns were entirely omitted. The music in this opera was composed by Smith, and contemporary journals speak of it in the highest terms. Garrick again produced the comedy at Drury Lane on Wednesday, November 23rd, 1763. The interlude was restored ; but it was very coldly received by a limited audience, and only acted once. The St. James's Chronicle, in a critique on this revival, describes it as "an odd romantic performance, more like a masque than a play, and presenting a lively picture of the ungoverned imagination of that great poet." It was then cut down to an afterpiece by Colman, under the title of A Fairy Tale (published in 8vo. 1764), the supernatural characters being alone retained, and produced in that form on November 26th, when it met with rather better success. Colman's alteration was again produced at the Haymarket Theatre on July 18th, 1777, with some songs added from Garrick's version (printed in 8vo, 1777). The Fairy Prince (8vo. 1771), also, acted at Covent Garden Theatre in 1771, contains a very few lines taken from this play, and from the Merry Wives of Windsor.

The principle of the composition of the following comedy has exercised the ingenuity of several critics, but perhaps the great difficulties which surround all æsthetic commentary on this play arise in some measure from its unity of action and of purpose having been considered axiomatical. If, however, the subject is entered upon without any preconceived opinion formed upon the results of an examination of other plays of the great dramatist, and the drama be regarded as an anomaly not regulated by ordinary laws, the discussion is somewhat less intricate. In point of fact, our chief perplexity will consist in the necessity of disconnecting some particular action from the rest, and regarding it as a subsequent invention. The fairies, undoubtedly, constitute the main action. Remove them from the scene, and the play would be a mere skeleton adorned with a few narrow robes of exquisite poetry. How, or in what manner the poet formed his frame-work—

and a beautiful and graceful frame it is—is a
question accessible only to conjecture. The
permutations of Shakespeare's fancy were infi-
nite, and here, as elsewhere, they have resolved
themselves into a systematic whole.

The Midsummer-Night's Dream contains the
sweetest poetry ever composed in any language;
a galaxy of music in words. It influenced the
fancy of Fletcher and Milton ; and its production has become an era in the history of English
poetical composition. It is difficult to ap-
preciate, impossible to delineate, the wonderful
effort of art by which the fairies are enabled to
be accepted as the chief actors in a material
comedy, without interfering with its perfect con-
gruity ; rendering the present drama the most
successful combination of the kind in our own
or in any language. Although a finished
dramatic piece, it is unquestionably better fitted
for the closet than the stage ; yet the portion
appropriated to the hard-handed men of Athens
is, in itself, an admirable farce : joined with the
action of the fairies, it becomes an artistic
comedy. The play is adapted to the stage by
the introduction of the clowns. Deprived of
the latter, it would have partaken of the character of a masque, and, like Comus, would not
have been appreciated by a common audience.

THE WIER BRAKE.

This picturesque locality, although it has been sadly injured of late years, still retains much of the character it must have possessed in the time of Shakespeare, and, indeed, the position of the wooded portion of the brake is now exactly as it was in the year 1599, as appears from a curious plan of that date. The following notice of the spot occurs in an account of the neighbourhood of Stratford-on-Avon which appeared in a newspaper a few years ago, but I have neglected to note the title and date of the journal,—" The Avon just below Stratford church is familiar to many visitors as they have stood on the wooden bridge and gazed on its stream flowing swiftly over the weedy bed and by the sedgy reedy banks. A footpath on the right or one on the left bank may be taken, and either will prove a pleasant route. The one on the left bank will lead towards the woody cliff, the Wier Brake, and through the tangled trees which tradition tells us formed the scene suggestive of the fairy freaks of the Midsummer Night's Dream ; but the right path, the lower one, will show this grand old pile of foliage sloping down to the cool calm margin of the lake-like stream to greater advantage still. The left bank, being the higher, commands the more extensive views, and especially many pleasant glimpses of the tower and spire of the church, which seem ever changing as the path and the river wind." Another interesting notice of the same locality is given by Mr. J. R. Wise in his elegant work on the Birthplace and its Neighbourhood, 1861, p. 80.—"We must now come back to the river across the fields, and we shall find ourselves at the Wier Brake, a wood which covers the high banks of the Avon at its first reach from the foot bridge. There is a tradition that this was the scene of the Midsummer Night's Dream. I am willing to believe it, for I do not like rooting up such old beliefs. The place is quite beautiful enough for such a scene; only do not ask me to believe too literally, for the the poet's mind wanders over all space, unconsciously gathering up all things it has ever seen or heard, and fusing them into a whole. The trees reach down from the high banks to the edge of the water, and the green fern plumes wave themselves whenever a little breeze steals through the branches ; and the people about here still believe, as in Shakespeare's time, that the fern seed, gathered with certain rites on Midsummer day, can make them invisible."

I have a suspicion that the above-mentioned "tradition" is one of a comparatively recent manufacture, but perhaps some one may be able to give me information respecting earlier notices of it. The communication of any such particulars would greatly oblige.